Hammett, Dashiell.
Woman in the dark.

DATE DUE

JAN 24 1995	DEC 02 2003
JUN 14 1995	FEB 12 2004
MAY 18 1996	OCT 22 2009
MAY 13 1997	MAR 03 2011
SEP 16 1997	JAN -2 2013
FEB 01 1998	NOV 17 2014
JUN 30 1998	JUL 09 2015
MAR 09 2000	JUL 15 2024
MAR 18 2000	
APR 30 2002	
SEP 19 2002	
MAR 09 2003	

GAYLORD   PRINTED IN U.S.A.

DISCARD

OCT 12 1988

WOMAN IN THE DARK

DASHIELL HAMMETT

With an Introduction by
Robert B. Parker

Woman in the Dark

A Novel of Dangerous Romance

 ALFRED A. KNOPF NEW YORK 1988

Library of Congress Cataloging-in-Publication Data

Hammett, Dashiell, 1894–1961.
  Woman in the dark.

  I. Title.
PS3515.A4347W6   1988   813'.52   88-45206
ISBN 0-394-57269-6

Manufactured in the United States of America
FIRST EDITION

Woman in the Dark was published in *Liberty* magazine in three installments on April 8, April 15, and April 22, 1933, and thus appeared after Dashiell Hammett had written all his novels but one. It is very much Hammett: the offbeat names (Brazil), the flat dialogue, the casually callous cops, the upper class bad guys, the decent low lifes (though suspicion of the wealthy was not peculiar to Hammett in 1933). And yet it also shows us Hammett's view of life in transition.

In *The Maltese Falcon*, Sam Spade recounts a story from his investigative past to Brigid O'Shaughnessy while they await Joel Cairo. Here is an abridged version. The words are Hammett's, the abridgement, mine.

A man named Flitcraft had left his real-estate-office, in Tacoma, to go to luncheon one day and had never returned. . . .

"He went like that," Spade said, "like a fist when you open your hand. . . . Well, that was in 1922. In 1927 I was with one of the big detective agencies in Seattle. Mrs. Flitcraft came in and told us somebody had seen a man in Spokane who looked a lot like her husband. I went over there. It was Flitcraft, all right. . . .

"Here's what had happened to him. Going to lunch he passed an office-building that was being put up—just the skeleton. A beam or something fell eight or ten stories down and smacked the sidewalk alongside him. It brushed pretty close to him, but didn't touch him, though a piece of the sidewalk was chipped off and flew up and hit his cheek. It only took a piece of skin off, but he still had the scar when I saw him. He rubbed it with his finger—well, affectionately—when he told me about it. He was scared stiff of course, he said, but he was more shocked than really frightened. He felt like somebody had taken the lid off life and let him look at the works."

Flitcraft had been a good citizen and a good husband and father, not by any outer compulsion, but simply because he was a man who was most comfortable in step with his surroundings. He had been raised that way. The people he knew were like that.

The life he knew was a clean orderly sane responsible affair. Now a falling beam had shown him that life was fundamentally none of these things. He, the good citizen-husband-father, could be wiped out between office and restaurant by the accident of a falling beam. He knew then that men died at haphazard like that, and lived only while blind chance spared them.

It was not, primarily, the injustice of it that disturbed him: he accepted that after the first shock. What disturbed him was the discovery that in sensibly ordering his affairs he had got out of step, and not into step, with life. He said he knew before he had gone twenty feet from the fallen beam that he would never know peace again until he had adjusted himself to this new glimpse of life. By the time he had eaten his luncheon he had found his means of adjustment. Life could be ended for him at random by a falling beam: he would change his life at random by simply going away. He loved his family, he said, as much as he supposed was usual, but he knew he was leaving them adequately provided for, and his love for them was not of the sort that would make absence painful.

"He went to Seattle that afternoon," Spade said, "and from there by boat to San Francisco. For a couple of years he wandered around and then drifted back to the Northwest, and settled in Spokane and got married. His second wife didn't look like the first, but they were more alike than they were different. You know, the kind of women that play fair games of golf and bridge and like new salad-recipes. He wasn't sorry for what he had done. It seemed reasonable enough to him. I don't think he even knew he had settled back naturally into the same groove he had jumped out of in Tacoma. But that's the part of it I always liked. He adjusted himself to beams falling, and then no more of them fell, and he adjusted himself to them not falling."

It seems like a time killer, idle talk while waiting. But of course it is not. It is Spade's motive spring. And it is this vision of an implacably random universe which informs nearly all of Hammett's work.

The men in this work are like Brazil. Sometimes they are detectives, sometimes not, but they are men who understand life as Spade understood it and expect whatever comes. They are men with few friends and no permanent social context. They have no family. Their allegiance is not to the law, but to something else, call it order, a sense of the way things ought to be. In many ways these men seem to be of the people. Indeed, it is occasionally fashionable to view Hammett's work from a Marxist perspective— though such a perspective usually requires one to chew more than he's bitten off. But these men are seemingly immune to the things that compel people. They do not

seem afraid of death. They seem able to resist the tempta-
tions of money and sex. They seem above pain, and un-
surprised by cruelty. They have no illusions. Brazil par-
ticularly seems to have muffled himself inside a great
calmness, as if nothing much mattered.

Yet like most of Hammett's men there is passion in
him, and it seethes under control only a little past the
I-don't-care. The passion often expresses itself in action
rather than in speech. The action is normally violent.
Woman in the Dark is more of a love story than Hammett
usually wrote.

It appeared two years after he began his lifelong rela-
tionship with Lillian Hellman, one year before publication
of his final novel, *The Thin Man*. And the fortuitous ending
and implied happily-ever-after for Brazil and Luise is more
sentimental than Hammett usually got.

"Hammett's style," Raymond Chandler once wrote,
"at its worst was as formalized as a page of Marius the
Epicurean; at its best it could say almost anything. I believe
this style, which does not belong to Hammett or to anybody, but is the American Language (and not even ex-
clusively that anymore), can say things he did not know
how to say, or feel the need of saying. In his hands it had no
overtones, left no echo, evoked no image beyond a distant
hill." Perhaps Hammett did not know how to write about
love or, until now, feel the need of it. To my eye the happy
ending seems a bit forced, as if Hammett, in order to bring
Brazil and Luise together after all, might have bent his

hard-eyed gaze away for a moment. I'm rather glad he did, in truth. I too am sentimental.

But if it worked all right here, it led him into a swamp that nearly drowned him in *The Thin Man*. It was as if Hammett could not accommodate Spade's Flitcraftian view of life with his impulse to write, at last, of love.

Whatever was at work in Hammett's soul, it is so that after *The Thin Man* in 1934 Hammett never wrote another novel, and when he died in 1961 he left only the fragment of one in progress, *Tulip*. In it he appeared to be trying to write something different, something that might integrate the conflicting impulses. Perhaps he tired. Perhaps he couldn't integrate the conflict.

Woman in the Dark is subtitled, after all, "A Novel of Dangerous Romance." It is a conjunction Hammett never quite tried before. It is a conjunction that works pretty well here. It never worked so well again, but for Hammett, the writer, nothing else did either.

Robert B. Parker

ONE

THE FLIGHT

Her right ankle turned under her and she fell. The wind blowing downhill from the south, whipping the trees beside the road, made a whisper of her exclamation and snatched her scarf away into the darkness. She sat up slowly, palms on the gravel pushing her up, and twisted her body sidewise to release the leg bent beneath her.

Her right slipper lay in the road close to her feet. When she put it on she found its heel was missing. She peered around, then began to hunt for the heel, hunting on hands and knees uphill into the wind, wincing a little when her right knee touched the road. Presently she gave it up and tried to break the heel off her left slipper, but could not. She replaced the slipper and rose with her back to the wind, leaning back against the wind's violence and the road's steep sloping. Her gown clung to her back, flew fluttering out before her. Hair lashed her cheeks. Walking high on the ball of her right foot to make up for the missing heel, she hobbled on down the hill.

At the bottom of the hill there was a wooden bridge, and, a hundred yards beyond, a sign that could not be read in the darkness marked a fork in the road. She halted there, not looking at the sign but around her, shivering now, though the wind had less force than it had had on the hill. Foliage to her left moved to show and hide yellow light. She took the left-hand fork.

In a little while she came to a gap in the bushes beside the road and sufficient light to show a path running off the road through the gap. The light came from the thinly curtained window of a house at the other end of the path.

She went up the path to the door and knocked. When there was no answer she knocked again.

A hoarse, unemotional masculine voice said: "Come in."

She put her hand on the latch; hesitated. No sound came from within the house. Outside, the wind was noisy everywhere. She knocked once more, gently.

The voice said, exactly as before: "Come in."

She opened the door. The wind blew it in sharply, her hold on the latch dragging her with it so that she had to cling to the door with both hands to keep from falling. The wind went past her into the room, to balloon curtains and scatter the sheets of a newspaper that had been on a table. She forced the door shut and, still leaning against it, said:

"I am sorry." She took pains with her words to make them clear notwithstanding her accent.

The man cleaning a pipe at the hearth said: "It's all right." His copperish eyes were as impersonal as his hoarse voice. "I'll be through in a minute." He did not rise from his chair. The edge of the knife in his hand rasped inside the brier bowl of his pipe.

She left the door and came forward, limping, examining him with perplexed eyes under brows drawn a little together. She was a tall woman and carried herself proudly, for all she was lame and the wind had tousled her hair and the gravel of the road had cut and dirtied her hands and bare arms and the red crepe of her gown.

She said, still taking pains with her words: "I must go to the railroad. I have hurt my ankle on the road. Eh?"

He looked up from his work then. His sallow, heavily featured face, under coarse hair nearly the color of his eyes, was not definitely hostile or friendly. He looked at the woman's face, at her torn skirt. He did not turn his head to call: "Hey, Evelyn."

A girl—slim maturing body in tan sport clothes, slender sunburned face with dark bright eyes and dark short hair—came into the room through a doorway behind him.

The man did not look around at her. He nodded at the woman in red and said: "This—"

The woman interrupted him: "My name is Luise Fischer."

The man said: "She's got a bum leg."

Evelyn's dark prying eyes shifted their focus from the woman to the man—she could not see his face—and to the woman again. She smiled, speaking hurriedly: "I'm just leaving. I can drop you at Mile Valley on my way home."

The woman seemed about to smile. Under her curious gaze Evelyn suddenly blushed, and her face became defiant while it reddened. The girl was pretty. Facing her, the woman had become beautiful; her eyes were long, heavily lashed, set well apart under a smooth broad brow, her mouth was not small but sensitively carved and mobile, and in the light from the open fire the surfaces of her face were as clearly defined as sculptured planes.

The man blew through his pipe, forcing out a small cloud of black powder. "No use hurrying," he said. "There's no train till six." He looked up at the clock on the mantelpiece. It said ten-thirty-three. "Why don't you help her with her leg?"

The woman said: "No, it is not necessary. I—" She put her weight on her injured leg and flinched, steadying herself with a hand on the back of a chair.

The girl hurried to her, stammering contritely: "I—I didn't think. Forgive me." She put an arm around the woman and helped her into the chair.

The man stood up to put his pipe on the mantelpiece, beside the clock. He was of medium height, but his sturdiness made him look shorter. His neck, rising from the V of a gray sweater, was short, powerfully muscled. Below the sweater he wore loose gray trousers and heavy brown shoes. He clicked his knife shut and put it in his pocket before turning to look at Luise Fischer.

Evelyn was on her knees in front of the woman, pulling off her right stocking, making sympathetic clucking noises, chattering nervously: "You've cut your knee too. Tch-tch-tch! And look how your ankle's swelling. You shouldn't've tried to walk all that distance in these slippers." Her body hid the woman's bare leg from the man. "Now, sit still and I'll fix it up in a minute." She pulled the torn red skirt down over the bare leg.

The woman's smile was polite. She said carefully: "You are very kind."

The girl ran out of the room.

The man had a paper package of cigarettes in his hand. He shook it until three cigarettes protruded half an inch and held them out to her. "Smoke?"

"Thank you." She took a cigarette, put it between her lips, and looked at his hand when he held a match to it. His hand was thick-boned, muscular, but not a laborer's. She looked through her lashes at his face while he was lighting his cigarette. He was younger than he had seemed at first glance—perhaps no older than thirty-two or -three—and his features, in the flare of his match, seemed less stolid than disciplined.

"Bang it up much?" His tone was merely conversational.

"I hope I have not." She drew up her skirt to look first at her ankle, then at her knee. The ankle was perceptibly though not greatly swollen; the knee was cut once deeply, twice less seriously. She touched the edges of the cuts gently with a forefinger. "I do not like pain," she said very earnestly.

Evelyn came in with a basin of steaming water, cloths, a roll of bandage, salve. Her dark eyes widened at the man and woman, but were hidden by lowered lids by the time their faces had turned toward her. "I'll fix it now. I'll have it all fixed in a minute." She knelt in front of the woman again, nervous hand sloshing water on the floor, body between Luise Fischer's leg and the man.

He went to the door and looked out, holding the door half a foot open against the wind.

The woman asked the girl bathing her ankle: "There is not a train before it is morning?" She pursed her lips thoughtfully.

"No."

The man shut the door and said: "It'll be raining in an hour." He put more wood on the fire, then stood—legs apart, hands in pockets, cigarette dangling from one side of his mouth—watching Evelyn attend to the woman's leg. His face was placid.

The girl dried the ankle and began to wind a bandage around it, working with increasing speed, breathing more rapidly now. Once more the woman seemed about to smile at the girl, but instead she said, "You are very kind."

The girl murmured: "It's nothing."

Three sharp knocks sounded on the door.

Luise Fischer started, dropped her cigarette, looked

swiftly around the room with frightened eyes. The girl did not raise her head from her work. The man, with nothing in his face or manner to show he had noticed the woman's fright, turned his face toward the door and called in his hoarse, matter-of-fact voice: "All right. Come in."

The door opened and a spotted Great Dane came in, followed by two tall men in dinner clothes. The dog walked straight to Luise Fischer and nuzzled her hand. She was looking at the two men who had just entered. There was no timidity, no warmth in her gaze.

One of the men pulled off his cap—it was a gray tweed, matching his topcoat—and came to her, smiling. "So this is where you landed?" His smile vanished as he saw her leg and the bandages. "What happened?" He was perhaps forty years old, well groomed, graceful of carriage, with smooth dark hair, intelligent dark eyes—solicitous at the moment—and a close-clipped dark mustache. He pushed the dog aside and took the woman's hand.

"It is not serious, I think." She did not smile. Her voice was cool. "I stumbled in the road and twisted my ankle. These people have been very—"

He turned to the man in the gray sweater, holding out his hand, saying briskly: "Thanks ever so much for taking care of Fräulein Fischer. You're Brazil, aren't you?"

The man in the sweater nodded. "And you'd be Kane Robson."

"Right." Robson jerked his head at the man who still stood just inside the door. "Mr. Conroy."

Brazil nodded. Conroy said, "How do you do," and

advanced toward Luise Fischer. He was an inch or two taller than Robson—who was nearly six feet himself—and some ten years younger, blond, broad-shouldered, and lean, with a beautifully shaped small head and remarkably symmetrical features. A dark overcoat hung over one of his arms and he carried a black hat in his hand. He smiled down at the woman and said: "Your idea of a lark's immense."

She addressed Robson: "Why have you come here?"

He smiled amiably, raised his shoulders a little. "You said you weren't feeling well and were going to lie down. When Helen went up to your room to see how you were, you weren't there. We were afraid you had gone out and something had happened to you." He looked at her leg, moved his shoulders again. "Well, we were right."

Nothing in her face responded to his smile. "I am going to the city," she told him. "Now you know."

"All right, if you want to"—he was good-natured—"but you can't go like that." He nodded at her torn evening dress. "We'll take you back home, where you can change your clothes and pack a bag and—" He turned to Brazil. "When's the next train?"

Brazil said: "Six." The dog was sniffing at his legs.

"You see," Robson said blandly, speaking to the woman again. "There's plenty of time."

She looked down at her clothes and seemed to find them satisfactory. "I go like this," she replied.

"Now, look here, Luise," Robson began again, quite

reasonably. "You've got hours before train time—time enough to get some rest and a nap and to—"

She said simply: "I have gone."

Robson grimaced impatiently, half humorously, and turned his palms out in a gesture of helplessness. "But what are you going to do?" he asked in a tone that matched the gesture. "You're not going to expect Brazil to put you up till train time and then drive you to the station?"

She looked at Brazil with level eyes and asked calmly: "Is it too much?"

Brazil shook his head carelessly. "Uh-uh."

Robson and Conroy turned together to look at Brazil. There was considerable interest in their eyes, but no visible hostility. He bore the inspection placidly.

Luise Fischer said coolly, with an air of finality: "So."

Conroy looked questioningly at Robson, who sighed wearily and asked: "Your mind's made up on this, Luise?"

"Yes."

Robson shrugged again, said: "You always know what you want." Face and voice were grave. He started to turn away toward the door, then stopped to ask: "Have you got enough money?" One of his hands went into the inner breast pocket of his dinner jacket.

"I want nothing," she told him.

"Right. If you want anything later, let me know. Come on, Dick."

He went to the door, opened it, twisted his head around to direct a brisk "Thanks, good night" at Brazil, and went out.

Conroy touched Luise Fischer's forearm lightly with three fingers, said "Good luck" to her, bowed to Evelyn and Brazil, and followed Robson out.

The dog raised his head to watch the two men go out. The girl Evelyn stared at the door with despairing eyes and worked her hands together. Luise Fischer told Brazil: "You will be wise to lock your door."

He stared at her for a long moment, brooding, and while no actual change seemed to take place in his expression, all his facial muscles stiffened. "No," he said finally, "I won't lock it."

The woman's eyebrows went up a little, but she said nothing. The girl spoke, addressing Brazil for the first time since Luise Fischer's arrival. Her voice was peculiarly emphatic. "They were drunk."

"They've been drinking," he conceded. He looked thoughtfully at her, apparently only then noticing her perturbation. "You look like a drink would do you some good."

She became confused. Her eyes evaded his. "Do—do you want one?"

"I think so." He looked inquiringly at Luise Fischer, who nodded and said: "Thank you."

The girl went out of the room. The woman leaned forward a little to look intently up at Brazil. Her voice was calm enough, but the deliberate slowness with which she spoke made her words impressive: "Do not make the mistake of thinking Mr. Robson is not dangerous."

He seemed to weigh this speech almost sleepily; then, regarding her with a slight curiosity, he said: "I've made an enemy?"

Her nod was sure.

He accepted that with a faint grin, offering her his cigarettes again, asking: "Have you?"

She stared through him as if studying some distant thing and replied slowly: "Yes, but I have lost a worse friend."

Evelyn came in, carrying a tray that held glasses, mineral water, and a bottle of whiskey. Her dark eyes, glancing from man to woman, were inquisitive, somewhat furtive. She went to the table and began to mix drinks.

Brazil finished lighting his cigarette and asked: "Leaving him for good?"

For the moment during which she stared haughtily at him it seemed that the woman did not intend to answer his question; but suddenly her face was distorted by an expression of utter hatred and she spit out a venomous "*Ja!*"

He set his glass on the mantelpiece and went to the door. He went through the motions of looking out into the night; yet he opened the door a bare couple of inches and shut it immediately, and his manner was so far from nervous that he seemed preoccupied with something else.

He turned to the mantelpiece, picked up his glass, and drank. Then, his eyes focused contemplatively on the lowered glass, he was about to speak when a telephone bell rang behind a door facing the fireplace. He opened the door, and as soon as he had passed out of sight his hoarse, unemotional voice could be heard. "Hello? . . . Yes . . . Yes, Nora . . . Just a moment." He re-entered the room, saying to the girl: "Nora wants to talk to you." He shut the bedroom door behind her.

Luise said: "You cannot have lived here long if you did not know Kane Robson before tonight."

"A month or so; but, of course, he was in Europe till he came back last week"—he paused—"with you." He picked up his glass. "Matter of fact, he is my landlord."

"Then you—" She broke off as the bedroom door opened. Evelyn stood in the doorway, hands to breast, and cried: "Father's coming—somebody phoned him I was here." She hurried across the room to pick up hat and coat from a chair.

Brazil said: "Wait. You'll meet him on the road if you go now. You'll have to wait till he gets here, then duck out back and beat him home while he's jawing at me. I'll stick your car down at the foot of the back road." He drained his glass and started for the bedroom door.

"But you won't"—her lip quivered—"won't fight with him? Promise me you won't."

"I won't." He went into the bedroom, returned almost immediately with a soft brown hat on his head and one of his arms in a raincoat. "It'll only take me five minutes." He went out the front door.

Luise Fischer said: "Your father does not approve?"

The girl shook her head miserably. Then suddenly

she turned to the woman, holding her hands out in an appealing gesture, lips—almost colorless—moving jerkily as her words tumbled out: "You'll be here. Don't let them fight. They mustn't."

The woman took the girl's hands and put them together between her own, saying: "I will do what I can, I promise you."

"He mustn't get in trouble again," the girl moaned. "He mustn't!"

The door opened and Brazil came in.

"That's done," he said cheerfully, and took off his raincoat, dropped it on a chair, and put his damp hat on it. "I left it at the end of the fence." He picked up the woman's empty glass and his own and went to the table. "Better slide out to the kitchen in case he pops in suddenly." He began to pour whiskey into the glasses.

The girl wet her lips with her tongue, said, "Yes, I guess so," indistinctly, smiled timidly, pleadingly, at Luise Fischer, hesitated, and touched his sleeve with her fingers. "You—you'll behave?"

"Sure." He did not stop preparing his drinks.

"I'll call you up tomorrow." She smiled at Luise Fischer and moved reluctantly toward the door.

Brazil gave the woman her glass, pulled a chair around to face her more directly, and sat down.

"Your little friend," the woman said, "she loves you very much."

He seemed doubtful. "Oh, she's just a kid," he said.

"But her father," she suggested, "he is not nice—eh?"

"He's cracked," he replied carelessly, then became thoughtful. "Suppose Robson phoned him?"

"Would he know?"

He smiled a little. "In a place like this everybody knows all about everybody."

"Then about me," she began, "you—"

She was interrupted by a pounding on the door that shook it on its hinges and filled the room with thunder. The dog came in, stiff-legged on its feet.

Brazil gave the woman a brief grim smile and called: "All right. Come in."

The door was violently opened by a medium-sized man in a glistening black rubber coat that hung to his ankles. Dark eyes set too close together burned under the down-turned brim of his gray hat. A pale bony nose jutted out above ragged, short-cut, grizzled mustache and beard. One fist gripped a heavy applewood walking stick.

"Where is my daughter?" this man demanded. His voice was deep, powerful, resounding.

Brazil's face was a phlegmatic mask. "Hello, Grant," he said.

The man in the doorway took another step forward. "Where is my daughter?"

The dog growled and showed its teeth. Luise Fischer said: "Franz!" The dog looked at her and moved its tail sidewise an inch or two and back.

Brazil said: "Evelyn's not here."

Grant glared at him. "Where is she?"

Brazil was placid. "I don't know."

"That's a lie!" Grant's eyes darted their burning gaze around the room. The knuckles of his hand holding the stick were white. "Evelyn!" he called.

Luise Fischer, smiling as if entertained by the bearded man's rage, said: "It is so, Mr. Grant. There is nobody else here."

He glanced briefly at her, with loathing in his mad eyes. "Bah! The strumpet's word confirms the convict's!" He strode to the bedroom door and disappeared inside.

Brazil grinned. "See? He's cracked. He always talks like that—like a guy in a bum book."

She smiled at him and said: "Be patient."

"I'm being," he said dryly.

Grant came out of the bedroom and stamped across to the rear door, opened it, and disappeared through it.

Brazil emptied his glass and put it on the floor beside his chair. "There'll be more fireworks when he comes back."

When the bearded man returned to the room, he stalked in silence to the front door, pulled it open, and, holding the latch with one hand, banging the ferrule of his walking stick on the floor with the other, roared at Brazil: "For the last time, I'm telling you not to have anything to do with my daughter! I shan't tell you again." He went out, slamming the door.

Brazil exhaled heavily and shook his head. "Cracked," he sighed. "Absolutely cracked."

Luise Fischer said: "He called me a strumpet. Do people here—"

He was not listening to her. He had left his chair and was picking up his hat and coat. "I want to slip down and see if she got away all right. If she gets home first she'll be O.K. Nora—that's her stepmother—will take care of her. But if she doesn't—I won't be long." He went out the back way.

Luise Fischer kicked off her remaining slipper and stood up, experimenting with her weight on her injured leg. Three tentative steps proved her leg stiff but serviceable. She saw then that her hands and arms were still dirty from the road and, exploring, presently found a bathroom opening off the bedroom. She hummed a tune to herself while she washed and, in the bedroom again, while she combed her hair and brushed her clothes—but broke off impatiently when she failed to find powder or lipstick. She was studying her reflection in a tall looking-glass when she heard the outer door opening.

Her face brightened. "I am here," she called, and went into the other room.

Robson and Conroy were standing inside the door.

"So you are, my dear," Robson said, smiling at her start of surprise. He was paler than before and his eyes were glassier, but he seemed otherwise unchanged. Conroy, however, was somewhat disheveled; his face was flushed and he was obviously rather drunk.

The woman had recovered composure. "What do you want?" she demanded bluntly.

Robson looked around. "Where's Brazil?"

"What do you want?" she repeated.

He looked past her at the open bedroom door, grinned, and crossed to it. When he turned from the empty room she sneered at him. Conroy had gone to the fireplace, where the Great Dane was lying, and was standing with his back to the fire, watching them.

Robson said: "Well, it's like this, Luise: you're going back home with me."

She said: "No."

He wagged his head up and down, grinning.

"I haven't got my money's worth out of you yet." He took a step toward her.

She retreated to the table, caught up the whiskey bottle by its neck. "Do not touch me!" Her voice, like her face, was cold with fury.

The dog rose, growling.

Robson's dark eyes jerked sidewise to focus on the dog, then on Conroy—and one eyelid twitched—then on the woman again.

Conroy—with neither tenseness nor furtiveness to alarm woman or dog—put his right hand into his overcoat pocket, brought out a black pistol, put its muzzle close behind one of the dog's ears, and shot the dog through the head. The dog tried to leap, fell on its side; its legs stirred feebly. Conroy, smiling foolishly, returned the pistol to his pocket.

Luise Fischer spun around at the sound of the shot. Screaming at Conroy, she raised the bottle to hurl it. But Robson caught her wrist with one hand, wrenched the bottle away with the other. He was grinning, saying, "No, no, my sweet," in a bantering voice.

He put the bottle on the table again, but kept his grip on her wrist.

The dog's legs stopped moving.

Robson said: "All right. Now, are you ready to go?"

She made no attempt to free her wrist. She drew herself up straight and said very seriously: "My friend, you do not know me yet if you think I am going with you."

Robson chuckled. "You don't know me if you think you're not," he told her.

The front door opened and Brazil came in. His sallow face was phlegmatic, though there was a shade of annoyance in his eyes. He shut the door carefully behind him, then addressed his guests. His voice was that of one who complains without anger. "What the hell is this?" he asked. "Visitors' day? Am I supposed to be running a roadhouse?"

Robson said: "We are going now. Fräulein Fischer's going with us."

Brazil was looking at the dead dog, annoyance deepening in his copperish eyes. "That's all right if she wants to," he said indifferently.

The woman said: "I am not going."

Brazil was still looking at the dog. "That's all right

too," he muttered, and with more interest: "But who did this?" He walked over to the dog and prodded its head with his foot. "Blood all over the floor," he grumbled.

Then, without raising his head, without the slightest shifting of balance or stiffening of his body, he drove his right fist up into Conroy's handsome, drunken face.

Conroy fell away from the fist rigidly, with upbent knees, turning a little as he fell. His head and one shoulder struck the stone fireplace, and he tumbled forward, rolling completely over, face upward, on the floor.

Brazil whirled to face Robson.

Robson had dropped the woman's wrist and was trying to get a pistol out of his overcoat pocket. But she had flung herself on his arm, hugging it to her body, hanging with her full weight on it, and he could not free it, though he tore her hair with his other hand.

Brazil went around behind Robson, struck his chin up with a fist so he could slide his forearm under it across the taller man's throat. When he had tightened the forearm there and had his other hand wrapped around Robson's wrist, he said: "All right. I've got him."

Luise Fischer released the man's arm and fell back on her haunches. Except for the triumph in it, her face was as businesslike as Brazil's.

Brazil pulled Robson's arm up sharply behind his back. The pistol came up with it, and when the pistol was horizontal Robson pulled the trigger. The bullet went between his back and Brazil's chest, to splinter the corner of a bookcase in the far end of the room.

Brazil said: "Try that again, baby, and I'll break your arms. Drop it!"

Robson hesitated, let the pistol clatter down on the floor. Luise Fischer scrambled forward on hands and knees to pick it up. She sat on a corner of the table, holding the pistol in her hand.

Brazil pushed Robson away from him and crossed the room to kneel beside the man on the floor, feeling his pulse, running hands over his body, and rising with Conroy's pistol, which he thrust into a hip pocket.

Conroy moved one leg, his eyelids fluttered sleepily, and he groaned.

Brazil jerked a thumb at him and addressed Robson curtly: "Take him and get out."

Robson went over to Conroy, stooped to lift his head and shoulders a little, shook him, and said irritably: "Come on, Dick, wake up. We're going."

Conroy mumbled, "I'm a' ri'," and tried to lie down again.

"Get up, get up," Robson snarled, and slapped his cheeks.

Conroy shook his head and mumbled: "Do' wan'a."

Robson slapped the blond face again. "Come on, get up, you louse."

Conroy groaned and mumbled something unintelligible.

Brazil said impatiently: "Get him out anyway. The rain'll bring him around."

Robson started to speak, changed his mind, picked up his hat from the floor, put it on, and bent over the blond man again. He pulled him up into something approaching a sitting position, drew one limp arm over his shoulder, got a hand around Conroy's back and under his armpit, and rose, slowly lifting the other on unsteady legs beside him.

Brazil held the front door open. Half dragging, half carrying Conroy, Robson went out.

Brazil shut the door, leaned his back against it, and shook his head in mock resignation.

Luise Fischer put Robson's pistol down on the table and stood up. "I am sorry," she said gravely. "I did not mean to bring to you all this—"

He interrupted her carelessly: "That's all right." There was some bitterness in his grin, though his tone remained careless. "I go on like this all the time. God! I need a drink."

She turned swiftly to the table and began to fill glasses.

He looked her up and down reflectively, sipped, and asked: "You walked out just like that?"

She looked down at her clothes and nodded yes.

He seemed amused. "What are you going to do?"

"When I go to the city? I shall sell these things"—she moved her hands to indicate her rings—"and then—I do not know."

"You mean you haven't any money at all?" he demanded.

"That is it," she replied coolly.

"Not even enough for your ticket?"

She shook her head no, raised her eyebrows a little, and her calmness was almost insolence. "Surely that is a small amount you can afford to lend me."

"Sure," he said, and laughed. "But you're a pip."

She did not seem to understand him.

He drank again, then leaned forward. "Listen, you're going to look funny riding the train like that." He flicked two fingers at her gown. "Suppose I drive you in and I've got some friends that'll put you up till you get hold of some clothes you can go out in?"

She studied his face carefully before replying: "If it is not too much trouble for you."

"That's settled, then," he said. "Want to catch a nap first?"

He emptied his glass and went to the front door, where he made a pretense of looking out at the night.

As he turned from the door he caught her expression, though she hastily put the frown off her face. His smile, voice were mockingly apologetic: "I can't help it. They had me away for a while—in prison, I mean—and it did that to me. I've got to keep making sure I'm not locked in." His smile became more twisted. "There's a name for it—claustrophobia—and that doesn't make it any better."

"I am sorry," she said. "Was it—very long ago?"

"Plenty long ago when I went in," he said dryly, "but only a few weeks ago that I got out. That's what I came up here for—to try to get myself straightened out, see how I stood, what I wanted to do."

"And?" she said softly.

"And what? Have I found out where I stand, what I want to do? I don't know." He was standing in front of her, hands in pockets, glowering down at her. "I suppose I've just been waiting for something to turn up, something I could take as a sign which way I was to go. Well, what turned up was you. That's good enough. I'll go along with you."

He took his hands from his pockets, leaned down, lifted her to her feet, and kissed her savagely.

For a moment she was motionless. Then she squirmed out of his arms and struck at his face with curved fingers. She was white with anger.

He caught her hand, pushed it down carelessly, and growled: "Stop it. If you don't want to play you don't want to play, that's all."

"That is exactly all," she said furiously.

"Fair enough." There was no change in his face, none in his voice.

Presently she said: "That man—your little friend's father—called me a strumpet. Do people here talk very much about me?"

He made a deprecatory mouth. "You know how it is. The Robsons have been the big landowners, the local gentry, for generations, and anything they do is big news. Everybody knows everything they do, and so—"

"And what do they say about me?"

He grinned. "The worst, of course. What do you expect? They know him."

"And what do you think?"

"About you?"

She nodded. Her eyes were intent on his.

"I can't very well go around panning people," he said, "only I wonder why you ever took up with him. You must've seen him for the rat he is."

"I did not altogether," she said simply. "And I was stranded in a little Swiss village."

"Actress?"

She nodded. "Singer."

The telephone bell rang.

He went unhurriedly into the bedroom. His unemotional voice came out: "Hello? . . . Yes, Evelyn . . . Yes." There was a long pause. "Yes; all right, and thanks."

He returned to the other room as unhurriedly as he had left, but at the sight of him Luise Fischer half rose from the table. His face was pasty, yellow, glistening with sweat on forehead and temples, and the cigarette between the fingers of his right hand was mashed and broken.

"That was Evelyn. Her father's justice of the peace. Conroy's got a fractured skull—dying. Robson just phoned he's going down to swear out a warrant. That damned fireplace. I can't live in a cell again!"

TWO

THE POLICE CLOSE IN

L uise came to him with her hands out. "But you are not to blame. They can't—"

"You don't get it," his monotonous voice went on. He turned away from her toward the front door, walked mechanically. "This is what they sent me up for the other time. It was a drunken free-for-all in a roadhouse, with bottles and everything, and a guy died. I couldn't say they were wrong in tying it on me." He opened the door, made his automatic pretense of looking out, shut the door, and moved back toward her.

"It was manslaughter that time. They'll make it murder if this guy dies. See? I'm on record as a killer." He put a hand up to his chin. "It's airtight."

"No, no." She stood close to him and took one of his hands. "It was an accident that his head struck the fireplace. I can tell them that. I can tell them what brought it all about. They cannot—"

He laughed with bitter amusement, and quoted Grant: " 'The strumpet's word confirms the convict's.' "

She winced.

"That's what they'll do to me," he said, less monotonously now. "If he dies I haven't got a chance. If he doesn't they'll hold me without bail till they see how it's coming out—assault with intent to kill or murder. What good'll your word be? Robson's mistress leaving him with me? Tell the truth and it'll only make it worse. They've got me"—his voice rose—"and I can't live in a cell again!" His eyes jerked around toward the door. Then he raised his head with a rasping noise in his throat that might have been a laugh. "Let's get out of here. I'll go screwy indoors tonight."

"Yes," she said eagerly, putting a hand on his shoulder, watching his face with eyes half frightened, half pitying. "We will go."

"You'll need a coat." He went into the bedroom.

She found her slippers, put on the right one, and held the left one out to him when he returned. "Will you break off the heel?"

He draped the rough brown overcoat he carried over her shoulders, took the slipper from her, and wrenched off the heel with a turn of his wrist. He was at the front door by the time she had her foot in the slipper.

She glanced swiftly once around the room and followed him out. . . .

.   .   .

She opened her eyes and saw daylight had come. Rain no longer dabbled the coupé's windows and windshield, and the automatic wiper was still. Without moving, she looked at Brazil. He was sitting low and lax on the seat beside her, one hand on the steering wheel, the other holding a cigarette on his knee. His sallow face was placid and there was no weariness in it. His eyes were steady on the road ahead.

"Have I slept long?" she asked.

He smiled at her. "An hour this time. Feel better?" He raised the hand holding the cigarette to switch off the headlights.

"Yes." She sat up a little, yawning. "Will we be much longer?"

"An hour or so." He put a hand in his pocket and offered her cigarettes.

She took one and leaned forward to use the electric lighter in the dashboard. "What will you do?" she asked when the cigarette was burning.

"Hide out till I see what's what."

She glanced sidewise at his placid face, said: "You too feel better."

He grinned somewhat shamefacedly. "I lost my head back there, all right."

She patted the back of his hand once, gently, and they rode in silence for a while. Then she asked: "We are going to those friends of whom you spoke?"

"Yes."

A dark coupé with two uniformed policemen in it came toward them, went past. The woman looked sharply at Brazil. His face was expressionless.

She touched his hand again, approvingly.

"I'm all right outdoors," he explained. "It's walls that get me."

She screwed her head around to look back. The policemen's car had passed out of sight.

Brazil said: "They didn't mean anything." He lowered the window on his side and dropped his cigarette out. Air blew in, fresh and damp. "Want to stop for coffee?"

"Had we better?"

An automobile overtook them, crowded them to the edge of the road in passing, and quickly shot ahead. It was a black sedan traveling at the rate of sixty-five or more miles an hour. There were four men in it, one of whom looked back at Brazil's car.

Brazil said: "Maybe it'd be safer to get under cover as soon as we can; but if you're hungry—"

"No; I too think we should hurry."

The black sedan disappeared around a bend in the road.

"If the police should find you, would"—she hesitated—"would you fight?"

"I don't know," he said gloomily. "That's what's the matter with me. I never know ahead of time what I'll do." He lost some of his gloominess. "There's no use worrying. I'll be all right."

They rode through a crossroads settlement of a dozen houses, bumped over railroad tracks, and turned into a long straight stretch of road paralleling the tracks. Halfway down the level stretch, the sedan that had passed them was stationary on the edge of the road. A policeman stood beside it—between it and his motorcycle—and stolidly wrote on a leaf of a small book while the man at the sedan's wheel talked and gestured excitedly.

Luise Fischer blew breath out and said: "Well, they were not police."

Brazil grinned.

Neither of them spoke again until they were riding down a suburban street. Then she said: "They—your friends—will not dislike our coming to them like this?"

"No," he replied carelessly; "they've been through things themselves."

The houses along the suburban street became cheaper and meaner, and presently they were in a shabby city street where grimy buildings with cards saying "Flats to Let" in their windows stood among equally grimy factories and warehouses. The street into which Brazil after a little while steered the car was only slightly less dingy, and the rental signs were almost as many.

He stopped the car in front of a four-story red brick building with broken brownstone steps. "This is it," he said, opening the door.

She sat looking at the building's unlovely face until he came around and opened the door on her side. Her face was inscrutable. Three dirty children stopped playing with the skeleton of an umbrella to stare at her as she went with him up the broken steps.

The street door opened when he turned the knob, letting them into a stuffy hallway where a dim light illuminated stained wallpaper of a once-vivid design, ragged carpet, and a worn brassbound staircase.

"Next floor," he said, and went up the stairs behind her.

Facing the head of the stairs was a door shiny with new paint of a brown peculiarly unlike any known wood. Brazil went to this door and pushed the bell button four times—long, short, long, short. The bell rang noisily just inside the door.

After a moment of silence, vague rustling noises came through the door, followed by a cautious masculine voice: "Who's there?"

Brazil put his head close to the door and kept his voice low: "Brazil."

The fastenings of the door rattled, and it was opened by a small, wiry blond man of about forty in crumpled green cotton pajamas. His feet were bare. His hollow-cheeked and sharp-featured face wore a cordial smile, and his voice was cordial. "Come in, kid," he said. "Come in." His small, pale eyes appraised Luise Fischer from head to foot while he was stepping back to make way for them.

Brazil put a hand on the woman's arm and urged her forward, saying: "Miss Fischer, this is Mr. Link."

Link said, "Pleased to meet you," and shut the door behind them.

Luise Fischer bowed.

Link slapped Brazil on the shoulder. "I'm glad to see you, kid. We were wondering what had happened to you. Come on in."

He led them into a living room that needed airing. There were articles of clothing lying around, sheets of newspaper here and there, a few not quite empty glasses and coffee cups, and a great many cigarette stubs. Link took a vest off a chair, threw it across the back of another, and said: "Take off your things and set down, Miss Fischer."

A very blonde full-bodied woman in her late twenties said, "My God, look who's here!" from the doorway and ran to Brazil with wide arms, hugged him violently, kissed him on the mouth. She had on a pink wrapper over a pink silk nightgown and green mules decorated with yellow feathers.

Brazil said, "Hello, Fan," and put his arms around her. Then, turning to Luise Fischer, who had taken off her coat: "Fan, this is Miss Fischer, Mrs. Link."

Fan went to Luise Fischer with her hand out. "Glad to know you," she said, shaking hands warmly. "You look tired, both of you. Sit down and I'll get you some break-fast, and maybe Donny'll get you a drink after he covers up his nakedness."

Luise Fischer said, "You are very kind," and sat down.

Link said, "Sure, sure," and went out.

Fan asked: "Been up all night?"

"Yes," Brazil said. "Driving most of it." He sat down on the sofa.

She looked sharply at him. "Anything the matter you'd just as lief tell me about?"

He nodded. "That's what we came for."

Link, in bathrobe and slippers now, came in with a bottle of whiskey and some glasses.

Brazil said: "The thing is, I slapped a guy down last night and he didn't get up."

"Hurt bad?"

Brazil made a wry mouth. "Maybe dying."

Link whistled, said: "When you slap 'em, boy, they stay slapped."

"He cracked his head on the fireplace," Brazil explained. He scowled at Link.

Fan said: "Well, there's no sense worrying about it now. The thing to do is get something in your stomachs and get some rest. Come on, Donny, pry yourself loose from some of that booze." She beamed on Luise Fischer. "You just sit still and I'll have some breakfast in no time at all." She hurried out of the room.

Link, pouring whiskey, asked: "Anybody see it?"

Brazil nodded. "Uh-huh—the wrong people." He sighed wearily. "I want to hide out a while, Donny, till I see how it's coming out."

"This dump's yours," Link said. He carried glasses of whiskey to Luise Fischer and Brazil. He looked at the woman whenever she was not looking at him.

Brazil emptied his glass with a gulp.

Luise Fischer sipped and coughed.

"Want a chaser?" Link asked.

"No, I thank you," she said. "This is very good. I caught a little cold from the rain."

She held the glass in her hand, but did not drink again.

Brazil said: "I left my car out front. I ought to bury it."

"I'll take care of that, kid," Link promised.

"And I'll want somebody to see what's happening up Mile Valley way."

Link wagged his head up and down. "Harry Klaus is the mouthpiece for you. I'll phone him."

"And we both want some clothes."

Luise Fischer spoke: "First I must sell these rings."

Link's pale eyes glistened. He moistened his lips and said: "I know the—"

"That can wait a day," Brazil said. "They're not hot, Donny. You don't have to fence them."

Donny seemed disappointed.

The woman said: "But I have no money for clothes until—"

Brazil said: "We've got enough for that."

Donny, watching the woman, addressed Brazil: "And you know I can always dig up some for you, kid."

"Thanks. We'll see." Brazil held out his empty glass, and when it had been filled said: "Hide the car, Donny."

"Sure." The blond man went to the telephone in an alcove and called a number.

Brazil emptied his glass. "Tired?" he asked.

She rose, went over to him, took the whiskey glass out of his hand, and put it on the table with her own, which was still almost full.

He chuckled, asked: "Had enough trouble with drunks last night?"

"Yes," she replied, not smiling, and returned to her chair.

Donny was speaking into the telephone: "Hello, Duke? . . . Listen; this is Donny. There's a ride standing outside my joint." He described Brazil's coupé. "Will you stash it for me? . . . Yes . . . Better switch the plates too. . . . Yes, right away, will you? . . . Right." He hung up the receiver and turned back to the others, saying: "*Voily!*"

"Donny!" Fan called from elsewhere in the flat.

"Coming!" He went out.

Brazil leaned toward Luise Fischer and spoke in a low voice: "Don't give him the rings."

She stared at him in surprise. "But why?"

"He'll gyp you to hell and gone."

"You mean he will cheat me?"

He nodded, grinning.

"But you say he is your friend. You are trusting him now."

"He's O.K. on a deal like this," he assured her. "He'd

never turn anybody up. But dough's different. Anyhow, even if he didn't trim you, anybody he sold them to would think they were stolen and wouldn't give half of what they're worth."

"Then he is a—" She hesitated.

"A crook. We were cellmates a while."

She frowned and said: "I do not like this."

Fan came to the door, smiling, and said: "Breakfast is served."

In the passageway Brazil turned and took a tentative step toward the front door, but checked himself when he caught Luise Fischer's eye and, grinning a bit sheepishly, followed her and the blonde woman into the dining room.

Fan would not sit down with them. "I can't eat this early," she told Luise Fischer. "I'll get you a hot bath ready and fix your bed, because I know you're all in and'll be ready to fall over as soon as you're done."

She went out, paying no attention to Luise Fischer's polite remonstrances.

Donny stuck a fork into a small sausage and said: "Now about them rings. I can—"

"That can wait," Brazil said. "We've got enough to go on a while."

"Maybe; but it's just as well to have a getaway stake ready in case you need it all of a sudden." Donny put the sausage into his mouth. "And you can't have too big a one."

He chewed vigorously. "Now, for instance, you take the case of Shuffling Ben Devlin. You remember Ben? He was in the carpenter shop. Remember? The big guy with the gam?"

"I remember," Brazil replied without enthusiasm.

Donny stabbed another sausage. "Well, Ben was in a place called Finehaven once and—"

"He was in a place called the pen when we knew him," Brazil said.

"Sure; that's what I'm telling you. It was all on account of Ben thought—"

Fan came in. "Everything's ready whenever you are," she told Luise Fischer.

Luise Fischer put down her coffee cup and rose. "It is a lovely breakfast," she said, "but I am too tired to eat much."

As she left the room Donny was beginning again: "It was all on account of—"

Fan took her to a room in the rear of the flat where there was a wide wooden bed with smooth white covers turned down. A white nightgown and a red wrapper lay on the bed. On the floor there was a pair of slippers. The blonde woman halted at the door and gestured with one pink hand. "If there's anything else you need, just sing out. The bathroom's just across the hall and I turned the water on."

"Thank you," Luise Fischer said; "you are very kind. I am imposing on you most—"

Fan patted her shoulder. "No friend of Brazil's can ever impose on me, darling. Now, you get your bath and a good sleep, and if there's anything you want, yell." She went out and shut the door.

Luise Fischer, standing just inside the door, looked slowly, carefully around the cheaply furnished room, and then, going to the side of the bed, began to take off her clothes. When she had finished she put on the red wrapper and the slippers and, carrying the nightgown over her arm, crossed the hallway to the bathroom. The bathroom was warm with steam. She ran cold water into the tub while she took the bandages off her knee and ankle.

After she had bathed she found fresh bandages in the cabinet over the basin, and rewrapped her knee but not her ankle. Then she put on nightgown, wrapper, and slippers, and returned to the bedroom. Brazil was there, standing with his back to her, looking out a window.

He did not turn around. Smoke from his cigarette drifted back past his head.

She shut the door slowly and leaned against it, the faintest of contemptuous smiles curving her mobile lips.

He did not move.

She went slowly to the bed and sat on the side farthest from him. She did not look at him but at a picture of a horse on the wall. Her face was proud and cold. She said: "I am what I am, but I pay my debts." This time the deliberate calmness of her voice was insolence. "I brought this trouble to you. Well, now, if you can find any use for me—" She shrugged.

He turned from the window without haste. His cop-

perish eyes, his face were expressionless. He said: "O.K."
He rubbed the fire of his cigarette out in an ashtray on the
dressing table and came around the bed to her.

She stood up straight and tall, awaiting him.

He stood close to her for a moment, looking at her
with eyes that weighed her beauty as impersonally as if she
had been inanimate. Then he pushed her head back rudely
and kissed her.

She made neither sound nor movement of her own,
submitting completely to his caress, and when he released
her and stepped back, her face was as unaffected, as mask-
like, as his.

He shook his head slowly. "No, you're no good at your
job." And suddenly his eyes were burning and he had her
in his arms and she was clinging to him and laughing softly
in her throat while he kissed her mouth and cheeks and
eyes and forehead.

Donny opened the door and came in. He leered know-
ingly at them as they stepped apart, and said: "I just
phoned Klaus. He'll be over as soon's he's had breakfast."

"O.K.," Brazil said.

Donny, still leering, withdrew, shutting the door.

"Who is this Klaus?" Luise Fischer asked.

"Lawyer," Brazil replied absent-mindedly. He was
scowling thoughtfully at the floor. "I guess he's our best
bet, though I've heard things about him that—" He broke
off impatiently. "When you're in a jam you have to take
your chances." His scowl deepened. "And the best you can
expect is the worst of it."

She took his hand and said earnestly: "Let us go away from here. I do not like these people. I do not trust them."

His face cleared and he put an arm around her again, but abruptly turned his attention to the door when a bell rang beyond it.

There was a pause; then Donny's guarded voice could be heard asking: "Who is it?"

The answer could not be heard.

Donny's voice, raised a little: "Who?"

Nothing was heard for a short while after that. The silence was broken by the creaking of a floorboard just outside the bedroom door. The door was opened by Donny. His pinched face was a caricature of alertness. "Bulls," he whispered. "Take the window." He was swollen with importance.

Brazil's face jerked around to Luise Fischer.

"Go!" she cried, pushing him toward the window. "I will be all right."

"Sure," Donny said; "me and Fan'll take care of her. Beat it, kid, and slip us the word when you can. Got enough dough?"

"Uh-huh." Brazil was kissing Luise Fischer.

"Go, go!" she gasped.

His sallow face was phlegmatic. He was laconic. "Be seeing you," he said, and pushed up the window. His foot was over the sill by the time the window was completely raised. His other foot followed the first immediately, and, turning on his chest, he lowered himself, grinning cheerfully at Luise Fischer for an instant before he dropped out of sight.

She ran to the window and looked down. He was rising from among weeds in the unkempt back yard. His head turned quickly from right to left. Moving with a swiftness that seemed mere unhesitancy, he went to the left-hand fence, up it, and over into the next-door yard.

Donny took her arm and pulled her from the window. "Stay away from there. You'll tip his mitt. He's all right, though Christ help the copper he runs into—if they're close."

Something heavy was pounding on the flat's front door. A heavy, authoritative voice came through: "Open up!"

Donny sneered in the general direction of the front door. "I guess I better let 'em in or they'll be making toothpicks of my front gate." He seemed to be enjoying the situation.

She stared at him with blank eyes.

He looked at her, looked at the floor and at her again, and said defensively: "Look—I love the guy. I love him!"

The pounding on the front door became louder.

"I guess I better," Donny said, and went out.

Through the open window came the sound of a shot. She ran to the window and, hands on sill, leaned far out.

Fifty feet to the left, on the top of a fence that divided the long row of back yards from the alley behind, Brazil was poised, crouching. As Luise Fischer looked, another shot sounded and Brazil fell down out of sight into the alley behind the fence. She caught her breath with a sob.

The pounding on the flat's front door suddenly stopped. She drew her head in through the window. She took her hands from the sill. Her face was an automaton's. She pulled the window down without seeming conscious of what she was doing, and was standing in the center of the room looking critically at her fingernails when a tired-faced huge man in wrinkled clothes appeared in the doorway.

He asked: "Where's he at?"

She looked up at him from her fingernails as she had looked at her fingernails. "Who?"

He sighed wearily. "Brazil." He went to a closet door, opened it. "You the Fischer woman?" He shut the door and moved toward the window, looking around the room, not at her, with little apparent interest.

"I am Luise Fischer," she said to his back.

He raised the window and leaned out. "How's it, Tom?" he called to someone below. Whatever answer he received was inaudible in the room.

Luise Fischer put attentiveness off her face as he turned to her. "I ain't had breakfast yet," he said.

Donny's voice came through the doorway from another part of the flat: "I tell you I don't know where he's gone to. He just dropped the dame here and hightailed. He didn't tell me nothing. He—"

A metallic voice said, "I bet you!" disagreeably. There was the sound of a blow.

Donny's voice: "If I did know I wouldn't tell you, you big crum! Now sock me again."

The metallic voice: "If that's what you want." There was the sound of another blow.

Fan's voice, shrill with anger, screamed, "Stop that, you—" and ceased abruptly.

The huge man went to the bedroom door and called toward the front of the flat: "Never mind, Ray." He addressed Luise Fischer: "Get some clothes on."

"Why?" she asked coolly.

"They want you back in Mile Valley."

"For what?" She did not seem to think it was true.

"I don't know," he grumbled impatiently. "This ain't my job. We're just picking you up for them. Something about some rings that belonged to a guy's mother and disappeared from the house the same time you did."

She held up her hands and stared at the rings. "But they didn't. He bought them for me in Paris and—"

The huge man scowled wearily. "Well, don't argue with me about it. It's none of my business. Where was this fellow Brazil meaning to go when he left here?"

"I do not know." She took a step forward, holding out her hand in an appealing gesture. "Is he—"

"Nobody ever does," he complained, ignoring the question he had interrupted. "Get your clothes on." He held a hand out to her. "Better let me take care of the junk."

She hesitated, then slipped the rings from her fingers and dropped them into his hand.

"Shake it up," he said. "I ain't had breakfast yet." He went out and shut the door.

She dressed hurriedly in the clothes she had taken off a short while before, though she did not again put on the one stocking she had worn down from Brazil's house. When she had finished, she went quietly, with a backward glance at the closed door, to the window, and began slowly, cautiously, to raise the sash.

The tired-faced huge man opened the door. "Good thing I was peeping through the keyhole," he said patiently. "Now come on."

Fan came into the room behind him. Her face was very pink; her voice was shrill. "What're you picking on her for?" she demanded. "She didn't do anything. Why don't you—"

"Stop it, stop it," the huge man begged. His weariness seemed to have become almost unbearable. "I'm only a copper told to bring her in on a larceny charge. I got nothing to do with it, don't know anything about it."

"It is all right, Mrs. Link," Luise Fischer said with dignity. "It will be all right."

"But you can't go like that," Fan protested, and turned to the huge man. "You got to let her put on some decent clothes."

He sighed and nodded. "Anything, if you'll only hurry it up and stop arguing with me."

Fan hurried out.

Luise Fischer addressed the huge man: "He too is charged with larceny?"

He sighed. "Maybe one thing, maybe another," he said spiritlessly.

She said: "He has done nothing."

"Well, I haven't neither," he complained.

Fan came in with some clothes, a blue suit and hat, dark slippers, stockings, and a white blouse.

"Just keep the door open," the huge man said. He went out of the room and stood leaning against an opposite wall, where he could see the windows in the bedroom.

Luise Fischer changed her clothes, with Fan's assistance, in a corner of the room where they were hidden from him.

"Did they catch him?" Fan whispered.

"I do not know."

"I don't think they did."

"I hope they did not."

Fan was kneeling in front of Luise Fischer, putting on her stockings. "Don't let them make you talk till you've seen Harry Klaus," she whispered rapidly. "You tell them he's your lawyer and you got to see him first. We'll send him down and he'll get you out all right." She looked up abruptly. "You didn't cop them, did you?"

"Steal the rings?" Luise Fischer asked in surprise.

"I didn't think so," the blonde woman said. "So you won't have to—"

The huge man's weary voice came to them: "Come on—cut out the barbering and get into the duds."

Fan said: "Go take a run at yourself."

Luise Fischer carried her borrowed hat to the looking-glass and put it on; then, smoothing down the suit, looked at her reflection. The clothes did not fit her so badly as might have been expected.

Fan said: "You look swell."

The man outside the door said: "Come on."

Luise Fischer turned to Fan. "Goodbye, and I—"

The blonde woman put her arms around her. "There's nothing to say, and you'll be back here in a couple of hours. Harry'll show those saps they can't put anything like this over on you."

The huge man said: "Come on."

Luise Fischer joined him and they went toward the front of the flat.

As they passed the living-room door Donny, rising from the sofa, called cheerfully: "Don't let them worry you, baby. We'll—"

A tall man in brown put a hand over Donny's face and pushed him back on the sofa.

Luise Fischer and the huge man went out. A police-department automobile was standing in front of the house where Brazil had left his coupé. A dozen or more adults and children were standing around it, solemnly watching the door through which she came.

A uniformed policeman pushed some of them aside to make passageway for her and her companion and got into the car behind them. "Let her go, Tom," he called to the chauffeur, and they drove off.

The huge man shut his eyes and groaned softly. "God, I'm *schwach!*"

They rode seven blocks and halted in front of a square red brick building on a corner. The huge man helped her out of the automobile and took her between two large frosted globes into the building, and into a room where a bald fat man in uniform sat behind a high desk.

The huge man said: "It's that Luise Fischer for Mile Valley." He took a hand from a pocket and tossed her rings on the desk. "That's the stuff, I guess."

The bald man said: "Nice picking. Get the guy?"

"Hospital, I guess."

Luise Fischer turned to him: "Was he—was he badly hurt?"

The huge man grumbled: "I don't know about it. Can't I guess?"

The bald man called: "Luke!"

A thin, white-mustached policeman came in.

The fat man said: "Put her in the royal suite."

Luise Fischer said: "I wish to see my lawyer."

The three men looked unblinkingly at her.

"His name is Harry Klaus," she said. "I wish to see him."

Luke said: "Come back this way."

She followed him down a bare corridor to the far end, where he opened a door and stood aside for her to go through. The room into which the door opened was a small one furnished with cot, table, two chairs, and some magazines. The window was large, fitted with a heavy wire grating.

In the center of the room she turned to say again: "I wish to see my lawyer."

The white-mustached man shut the door and she could hear him locking it.

Two hours later he returned with a bowl of soup, some cold meat and a slice of bread on a plate, and a cup of coffee.

She had been lying on the cot, staring at the ceiling. She rose and faced him imperiously. "I wish to see—"

"Don't start that again," he said irritably. "We got nothing to do with you. Tell it to them Mile Valley fellows when they come for you."

He put the food on the table and left the room. She ate everything he had brought her.

It was late afternoon when the door opened again. "There you are," the white-mustached man said, and stood aside to let his companions enter. There were two of them, men of medium height, in dull clothes, one thick-chested and florid, the other less heavy, older.

The thick-chested, florid one looked Luise Fischer up and down and grinned admiringly at her. The other said: "We want you to come back to the Valley with us, Miss Fischer."

She rose from her chair and began to put on her hat and coat.

"That's it," the older of the two said. "Don't give us no trouble and we don't give you none."

She looked curiously at him.

They went to the street and got into a dusty blue sedan. The thick-chested man drove. Luise Fischer sat behind him, beside the older man. They retraced the route she and Brazil had taken that morning.

Once, before they left the city, she had said: "I wish to see my lawyer. His name is Harry Klaus."

The man beside her was chewing gum. He made noises with his lips, then told her, politely enough: "We can't stop now."

The man at the wheel spoke before she could reply. He did not turn his head. "How come Brazil socked him?"

Luise said quickly: "It was not his fault. He was—"

The older man, addressing the man at the wheel, interrupted her: "Let it alone, Pete. Let the D.A. do his own work."

Pete said: "Oke."

The woman turned to the man beside her. "Was—was Brazil hurt?"

He studied her face for a long moment, then nodded slightly. "Stopped a slug, I hear."

Her eyes widened. "He was shot?"

He nodded again.

She put both hands on his forearm. "How badly?"

He shook his head. "I don't know."

Her fingers dug into his arm. "Did they arrest him?"

"I can't tell you, miss. Maybe the District Attorney

wouldn't like me to." He smacked his lips over his gum-chewing.

"But, please!" she insisted. "I must know."

He shook his head again. "We ain't worrying you with a lot of questions. Don't be worrying us."

THREE

CONCLUSION

It was nearly nine o'clock by the dial on the dashboard, and quite dark, when Luise Fischer and her captors passed a large square building whose illuminated sign said "Mile Valley Lumber Co." and turned in to what was definitely a town street, though its irregularly spaced houses were not many. Ten minutes later the sedan came to rest at the curb in front of a gray public building. The driver got out. The other man held the door open for Luise. They took her into a ground-floor room in the gray building.

Three men were in the room. A sad-faced man of sixty-some years, with ragged white hair and mustache, was tilted back in a chair, with his feet on a battered yellowish desk. He wore a hat but no coat. A pasty-faced young blond man, straddling a chair in front of the filing cabinet on the other side of the room, was saying, "So the traveling salesman asked the farmer if he could put him up for the night and—" but broke off when Luise Fischer and her companions came in.

The third man stood with his back to the window. He was a slim man of medium height, not far past thirty, thin-lipped, pale, flashily dressed in brown and red. His collar was very tight. He advanced swiftly toward Luise Fischer, showing white teeth in a smile. "I'm Harry Klaus. They wouldn't let me see you down there, so I came on up to wait for you." He spoke rapidly and with assurance. "Don't worry. I've got everything fixed."

The storyteller hesitated, changed his position. The two men who had brought Luise Fischer up from the city looked at the lawyer with obvious disapproval.

Klaus smiled again with complete assurance. "You know she's not going to tell you anything at all till we've talked it over, don't you? Well, what the hell, then?"

The man at the desk said: "All right, all right." He looked at the two men standing behind the woman. "If Tuft's office is empty, let 'em use that."

"Thanks." Harry Klaus picked up a brown briefcase from a chair, took Luise Fischer's elbow in his hand, and turned her to follow the thick-chested, florid man.

He led them down the corridor a few feet to an office that was similar to the one they had just left. He did not go in with them. He said, "Come on back when you're finished," and, when they had gone in, slammed the door.

Klaus jerked his head at the door. "A lot of whittlers," he said cheerfully. "We'll stand them on their heads." He tossed his briefcase on the desk. "Sit down."

"Brazil?" she said. "He is—"

His shrug lifted his shoulders almost to his ears. "I don't know. Can't get anything out of these people."

"Then—?"

"Then he got away," he said.

"Do you think he did?"

He shrugged his shoulders again. "We can always hope."

"But one of those policemen told me he had been shot and—"

"That don't have to mean anything but that they hope they hit him." He put his hands on her shoulders and pushed her down into a chair. "There's no use of worrying about Brazil till we know whether we've got anything to worry about." He drew another chair up close to hers and sat in it. "Let's worry about you now. I want the works—no song and dance—just what happened, the way it happened."

She drew her brows together in a puzzled frown. "But you told me everything—"

"I told you everything was all fixed, and it is." He patted her knee. "I've got the bail all fixed so you can walk out of here as soon as they get through asking you questions. But we've got to decide what kind of answers you're going to give them." He looked sharply at her from under his hat brim. "You want to help Brazil, don't you?"

"Yes."

"That's the stuff." He patted her knee again, and his hand remained on it. "Now, give me everything, from the beginning."

"You mean from when I first met Kane Robson?"

He nodded.

She crossed her knees, dislodging his hand. Staring at the opposite wall as if not seeing it, she said earnestly: "Neither of us did anything wrong. It is not right that we should suffer."

"Don't worry." His tone was light, confident. "I'll get the pair of you out of it." He proffered her cigarettes in a shiny case.

She took a cigarette, leaned forward to hold its end to the flame from his lighter, and, still leaning forward, asked: "I will not have to stay here tonight?"

He patted her cheek. "I don't think so. It oughtn't to take them more than an hour to grill you." He dropped his hand to her knee. "And the sooner we get through here, the sooner you'll be through with them."

She took a deep breath and sat back in her chair. "There is not a lot to say," she began, pronouncing her words carefully so they were clear in spite of her accent. "I met him in a little place in Switzerland. I was without any money at all, any friends. He liked me and he was rich." She made a little gesture with the cigarette in her hand. "So I said yes."

Klaus nodded sympathetically and his fingers moved on her knee.

"He bought me clothes, those jewels, in Paris. They were not his mother's and he gave them to me."

The lawyer nodded again and his fingers moved again on her knee.

"He brought me over here then and"—she put the burning end of her cigarette on the back of his hand—"I stayed at his—"

Klaus had snatched his hand from her knee to his mouth, was sucking the back of his hand. "What's the matter with you?" he demanded indignantly, the words muffled by the hand to his mouth. He lowered the hand and looked at the burn. "If there's something you don't like, you can say so, can't you?"

She did not smile. "I no speak Inglis good," she said, burlesquing a heavy accent. "I stayed at his house for two weeks—not quite two weeks—until—"

"If it wasn't for Brazil, you could take your troubles to another lawyer!" He pouted over his burned hand.

"Until last night," she continued, "when I could stand him no longer. We quarreled and I left. I left just as I was, in evening clothes, with . . ."

She was finishing her story when the telephone bell rang. The attorney went to the desk and spoke into the telephone: "Hello? . . . Yes . . . Just a couple of minutes more . . . That's right. Thanks." He turned. "They're getting impatient."

She rose from her chair, saying: "I have finished. Then the police came and he escaped through the window and they arrested me about those rings."

"Did you do any talking after they arrested you?"

She shook her head. "They would not let me. Nobody would listen to me. Nobody cared."

A young man in blue clothes that needed pressing came up to Luise Fischer and Klaus as they left the courthouse. He took off his hat and tucked it under an arm. "Mith Fither, I'm from the Mile Valley *Potht*. Can you—"

Klaus, smiling, said: "There's nothing now. Look me up at the hotel in the morning and I'll give you a statement." He handed the reporter a card. He cleared his throat. "We're hunting food now. Maybe you'll tell us where to find it—and join us."

The young man's face flushed. He looked at the card in his hand and then up at the lawyer. "Thank you, Mithter Klauth, I'll be glad to. The Tavern'th jutht around the corner. It'th the only plathe that'th any good that'th open now."

He turned to indicate the south. "My name'th George Dunne."

Klaus shook his hand and said, "Glad to know you," Luise Fischer nodded and smiled, and they went down the street.

"How's Conroy?" Klaus asked.

"He hathn't come to yet," the young man replied. "They don't know yet how bad it ith."

"Where is he?"

"Thtill at Robthon'th. They're afraid to move him."

They turned the corner. Klaus asked: "Any news of Brazil?"

The reporter craned his neck to look past Luise Fischer at the lawyer. "I thought you'd know."

"Know what?"

"What—whatever there wath to know. Thith ith it."

He led them into a white-tiled restaurant. By the time they were seated at a table, the dozen or more people at counter and tables were staring at Luise Fischer and there was a good deal of whispering among them.

Luise Fischer, sitting in the chair Dunne had pulled out for her, taking one of the menus from the rack on the table, seemed neither disturbed by nor conscious of any-one's interest in her. She said: "I am very hungry."

A plump, bald-headed man with a pointed white beard, sitting three tables away, caught Dunne's eye as the young man went around to his chair, and beckoned with a jerk of his head.

Dunne said, "Pardon me—it'th my both," and went over to the bearded man's table.

Klaus said: "He's a nice boy."

Luise Fischer said: "We must telephone the Links. They have surely heard from Brazil."

Klaus pulled the ends of his mouth down, shook his

head. "You can't trust these county-seat telephone exchanges."

"But—"

"Have to wait till tomorrow. It's late anyhow." He looked at his watch and yawned. "Play this kid. Maybe he knows something."

Dunne came back to them. His face was flushed and he seemed embarrassed.

"Anything new?" Klaus asked.

The young man shook his head violently. "Oh, no!" he said with emphasis.

A waiter came to their table. Luise Fischer ordered soup, a steak, potatoes, asparagus, a salad, cheese, and coffee. Klaus ordered scrambled eggs and coffee, Dunne pie and milk.

When the waiter stepped back from the table, Dunne's eyes opened wide. He stared past Klaus. Luise Fischer turned her head to follow the reporter's gaze. Kane Robson was coming into the restaurant. Two men were with him. One of them—a fat, pale, youngish man— smiled and raised his hat.

Luise Fischer addressed Klaus in a low voice: "It's Robson."

The lawyer did not turn his head. He said, "That's all right," and held his cigarette case out to her.

She took a cigarette without removing her gaze from Robson. When he saw her, he raised his hat and bowed. Then he said something to his companions and, leaving them, came toward her. His face was pale; his dark eyes glittered.

She was smoking by the time he reached her table. He said, "Hello, darling," and sat in the empty chair facing her across the table. He turned his head to the reporter for an instant to say a careless "Hello, Dunne."

Luise Fischer said: "This is Mr. Klaus. Mr. Robson."

Robson did not look at the lawyer. He addressed the woman: "Get your bail fixed up all right?"

"As you see."

He smiled mockingly. "I meant to leave word that I'd put it up if you couldn't get it anywhere else, but I forgot."

There was a moment of silence. Then she said: "I shall send for my clothes in the morning. Will you have Ito pack them?"

"Your clothes?" He laughed. "You didn't have a stitch besides what you had on when I picked you up. Let your new man buy you new clothes."

Young Dunne blushed and looked at the tablecloth in embarrassment. Klaus's face was, except for the brightness of his eyes, expressionless.

Luise Fischer said softly: "Your friends will miss you if you stay away too long."

"Let them. I want to talk to you, Luise." He addressed Dunne impatiently: "Why don't you two go play in a corner somewhere?"

The reporter jumped from his chair, stammering: "Th-thertainly, Mr. Robthon."

Klaus looked questioningly at Luise Fischer. Her nod was barely perceptible. He rose and left the table with Dunne.

Robson said: "Come back with me and I'll call off all this foolishness about the rings."

She looked curiously at him. "You want me back, knowing I despise you?"

He nodded, grinning. "I can get fun out of even that."

She narrowed her eyes, studying his face. Then she asked: "How is Dick?"

His face and voice were gay with malice. "He's dying fast enough."

She seemed surprised. "You hate him?"

"I don't hate him—I don't love him. You and he were too fond of each other. I won't have any male and female parasites mixing like that."

She smiled contemptuously. "So. Then suppose I go back with you. What?"

"I explain to these people that it was all a mistake about the rings, that you really thought I had given them to you. That's all." He was watching her closely. "There's no bargaining about your boyfriend, Brazil. He takes what he gets."

Her face showed nothing of what she might be thinking. She leaned across the table a little toward him and spoke carefully: "If you were as dangerous as you think you are, I would be afraid to go back with you—I would rather go to prison. But I am not afraid of you. You should know by this time that you will never hurt me very much, that I can take very good care of myself."

"Maybe you've got something to learn," he said quickly; then, recovering his consciously matter-of-fact tone: "Well, what's the answer?"

"I am not a fool," she said. "I have no money, no friends who can help me. You have both, and I am not afraid of you. I try to do what is best for myself. First I try to get out of this trouble without you. If I cannot, then I come back to you."

"If I'll have you."

She shrugged her shoulders. "Yes, certainly that."

Luise Fischer and Harry Klaus reached the Links' flat late the next morning.

Fan opened the door for them. She put her arms around Luise Fischer. "See, I told you Harry would get you out all right." She turned to face the lawyer quickly and demanded: "You didn't let them hold her all night?"

"No," he said; "but we missed the last train and had to stay at the hotel."

They went into the living room.

Evelyn Grant rose from the sofa. She came to Luise Fischer, saying: "It's my fault. It's all my fault!" Her eyes were red and swollen. She began to cry again. "He had told me about Donny—Mr. Link—and I thought he'd come here and I tried to phone him and Papa caught me and told the police. And I only wanted to help him—"

From the doorway Donny snarled: "Shut up. Stop it. Pipe down." He addressed Klaus petulantly: "She's been doing this for an hour. She's got me screwy."

Fan said: "Lay off the kid. She feels bad."

Donny said: "She ought to." He smiled at Luise Fischer. "Hello, baby. Everything O.K.?"

She said: "How do you do? I think it is."

He looked at her hands. "Where's the rings?"

"We had to leave them up there."

"I told you!" His voice was bitter. "I told you you'd ought to let me sold them." He turned to Klaus. "Can you beat that?"

The lawyer did not say anything.

Fan had taken Evelyn to the sofa and was soothing her.

Luise Fischer asked: "Have you heard from—"

"Brazil?" Donny said before she could finish her question. He nodded. "Yep. He's O.K." He glanced over his shoulder at the girl on the sofa, then spoke rapidly in a low voice. "He's at the Hilltop Sanatorium, outside of town—supposed to have D.T.'s. You know he got plugged in the side. He's O.K., though—Doc Barry'll keep him under cover and fix him up good as new. He—"

Luise Fischer's eyes were growing large. She put a hand to her throat. "But he—Dr. Ralph Barry?" she demanded.

Donny wagged his head up and down. "Yes. He's a good guy. He'll—"

"But he is a friend of Kane Robson's!" she cried. "I met him there, at Robson's house." She turned to Klaus. "He was with him in the restaurant last night—the fat one."

The men stared at her.

She caught Klaus's arm and shook him. "That is why he was there last night—to see Kane—to ask him what he should do."

Fan and Evelyn had risen from the sofa and were listening.

Donny began: "Aw, maybe it's O.K. Doc's a good guy. I don't think he—"

"Cut it out!" Klaus growled. "This is serious—serious as hell." He scowled thoughtfully at Luise Fischer. "No chance of a mistake on this?"

"No."

Evelyn thrust herself between the two men to confront Luise Fischer. She was crying again, but was angry now.

"Why did you have to get him into all this? Why did you have to come to him with your troubles? It's your fault that they'll put him in prison—and he'll go crazy in prison! If it hadn't been for you, none of this would have happened. You—"

Donny touched Evelyn's shoulder. "I think I'll take a sock at you," he said.

She cringed away from him.

Klaus said: "For God's sake, let's stop this fiddledeedee and decide what we'd better do." He scowled at

Luise Fischer again. "Didn't Robson say anything to you about it last night?"

She shook her head.

Donny said: "Well, listen. We got to get him out of there. It don't—"

"That's easy," Klaus said with heavy sarcasm. "If he's in wrong there"—he shrugged—"it's happened already. We've got to find out. Can you get to see him?"

Donny nodded. "Sure."

"Then go. Wise him up—find out what the layout is."

Donny and Luise Fischer left the house by the back door, went through the yard to the alley behind, and down the alley for two blocks. They saw nobody following them.

"I guess we're in the clear," Donny said, and led the way down a cross street.

On the next corner there was a garage and repair shop. A small dark man was tinkering with an engine.

"Hello, Tony," Donny said. "Lend me a boat."

The dark man looked curiously at Luise Fischer while saying: "Surest thing you know. Take the one in the corner."

They got into a black sedan and drove away.

"It ain't far," Donny said. Then: "I'd like to pull him out of there."

Luise Fischer was silent.

After half an hour Donny turned the machine in to a road at the end of which a white building was visible. "That's her," he said.

After leaving the sedan in front of the building, they walked under a black-and-gold sign that said "Hilltop Sanatorium" into an office.

"We want to see Mr. Lee," Donny told the nurse at the desk. "He's expecting us."

She moistened her lips nervously and said: "It's two hundred and three, right near the head of the stairs."

They went up a dark flight of stairs to the second floor. "This is it," Donny said, halting. He opened the door without knocking and waved Luise Fischer inside.

Besides Brazil, lying in bed, his sallowness more pronounced than usual, there were two men in the room. One of them was the huge tired-faced man who had arrested Luise Fischer. He said: "I oughtn't to let you people see him."

Brazil half rose in bed and stretched a hand out toward Luise Fischer.

She went around the huge man to the bed and took Brazil's hand. "Oh, I'm sorry—sorry!" she murmured.

He grinned without pleasure. "Hard luck, all right. And I'm scared stiff of those damned bars."

She leaned over and kissed him.

The huge man said: "Come on, now. You got to get out. I'm liable to catch hell for this."

Donny took a step toward the bed. "Listen, Brazil. Is there—"

The huge man put out a hand and wearily pushed Donny back. "Go 'way. There's nothing for you to hang around here for." He put a hand on Luise Fischer's shoulder. "Go ahead, please, will you? Say goodbye to him now—and maybe you can see him afterwards."

She kissed Brazil again and stood up.

He said: "Look after her, will you, Donny?"

"Sure," Donny promised. "And don't let them worry you. I'll send Harry over to see you and—"

The huge man groaned. "Is this going to keep you all day?"

He took Luise Fischer's arm and put her and Donny out.

They went in silence down to the sedan, and neither spoke until they were entering the city again. Then Luise Fischer said: "Will you kindly lend me ten dollars?"

"Sure." Donny took one hand from the wheel, felt in his pants pocket, and gave her two five-dollar bills.

Then she said: "I wish to go to the railroad station."

He frowned. "What for?"

"I want to go to the railroad station," she repeated.

When they reached the station she got out of the sedan.

"Thank you very much," she said. "Do not wait. I will come over later."

Luise Fischer went into the railroad station and to the newsstand, where she bought a package of cigarettes. Then she went to a telephone booth, asked for long distance, and called a Mile Valley number.

"Hello, Ito? . . . Is Mr. Robson there? This is Fräulein Fischer. . . . Yes." There was a pause. "Hello, Kane . . . Well, you have won. You might have saved yourself the delay if you had told me last night what you knew. . . . Yes . . . Yes, I am."

She put the receiver on its prong and stared at it for a long moment. Then she left the booth, went to the ticket window, and said: "A ticket to Mile Valley—one-way—please."

The room was wide and high-ceilinged. Its furniture was Jacobean. Kane Robson was sprawled comfortably in a deep chair. At his elbow was a small table on which were a crystal-and-silver coffee service, a crystal-and-silver decanter—half full—some glasses, cigarettes, and an ashtray. His eyes glittered in the light from the fireplace.

Ten feet away, partly facing him, partly facing the fireplace, Luise Fischer sat, more erectly, in a smaller chair. She was in a pale negligee and had pale slippers on her feet.

Somewhere in the house a clock struck midnight. Robson heard it out attentively before he went on speaking: "And you are making a great mistake, my dear, in being too sure of yourself."

She yawned. "I slept very little last night," she said. "I am too sleepy to be frightened."

He rose, grinning at her. "I didn't get any either. Shall we take a look at the invalid before we turn in?"

A nurse—a scrawny middle-aged woman in white—came into the room, panting. "Mr. Conroy's recovering consciousness, I do believe," she said.

Robson's mouth tightened, and his eyes, after a momentary flickering, became steady. "Phone Dr. Blake," he said. "He'll want to know right away." He turned to Luise Fischer. "I'll run up and stay with him till she is through phoning."

Luise Fischer rose. "I'll go with you."

He pursed his lips. "I don't know. Maybe the excitement of too many people—the surprise of seeing you back here again—might not be good for him."

The nurse had left the room.

Ignoring Luise Fischer's laughter, he said: "No; you had better stay here, my dear."

She said: "I will not."

He shrugged. "Very well, but—" He went upstairs without finishing the sentence.

Luise Fischer went up behind him, but not with his speed. She arrived at the sickroom doorway, however, in time to catch the look of utter fear in Conroy's eyes, before they closed, as his bandaged head fell back on the pillow.

Robson, standing just inside the door, said softly: "Ah, he's passed out again." His eyes were unwary.

Her eyes were probing.

They stood there and stared at each other until the Japanese butler came to the door and said: "A Mr. Brazil to see Fräulein Fischer."

Into Robson's face little by little came the expression of one considering a private joke. He said: "Show Mr. Brazil into the living room. Fräulein Fischer will be down immediately. Phone the deputy sheriff."

Robson smiled at the woman. "Well?"

She said nothing.

"A choice?" he asked.

The nurse came in. "Dr. Blake is out, but I left word."

Luise Fischer said: "I do not think Mr. Conroy should be left alone, Miss George."

Brazil was standing in the center of the living room, balancing himself on legs spread far apart. He held his left arm tight to his side, straight down. He had on a dark overcoat that was buttoned high against his throat. His face was a ghastly yellow mask in which his eyes burned redly. He said through his teeth: "They told me you'd come back. I had to see it." He spit on the floor. "Strumpet!"

She stamped a foot. "Do not be a fool. I—" She broke off as the nurse passed the doorway. She said sharply: "Miss George, what are you doing?"

The nurse said: "Mr. Robson said he thought I might be able to reach Dr. Blake on the phone at Mrs. Webber's."

Luise Fischer turned, paused to kick off her slippers, and ran up the steps on stockinged feet. The door to Conroy's room was shut. She flung it open.

Robson was leaning over the sick man. His hands were on the sick man's bandaged head, holding it almost face down in the pillow.

His thumbs were pressing the back of the skull. All his weight seemed on his thumbs. His face was insane. His lips were wet.

Luise Fischer screamed, "Brazil!" and flung herself at Robson and clawed at his legs.

Brazil came into the room, lurching blindly, his left arm tight to his side. He swung his right fist, missed Robson's head by a foot, was struck twice in the face by Robson, did not seem to know it, and swung his right fist into Robson's belly. The woman's grip on Robson's ankles kept him from recovering his balance. He went down heavily.

The nurse was busy with her patient, who was trying to sit up in bed. Tears ran down his face. He was sobbing: "He stumbled over a piece of wood while he was helping me to the car, and he hit me on the head with it."

Luise Fischer had Brazil sitting up on the floor with his back to the wall, wiping his face with her handkerchief.

He opened one eye and murmured: "The guy was screwy, wasn't he?"

She put an arm around him and laughed with a cooing sound in her throat. "All men are."

Robson had not moved.

There was a commotion, and three men came in.

The tallest one looked at Robson and then at Brazil and chuckled.

"There's our lad that don't like hospitals," he said. "It's a good thing he didn't escape from a gymnasium or he might've hurt somebody."

Luise Fischer took off her rings and put them on the floor beside Robson's left foot.

A NOTE ABOUT THE AUTHOR

Dashiell Hammett was born in St. Marys County, Maryland, in 1894. He grew up in Philadelphia and Baltimore. He left school at fourteen and held all kinds of jobs thereafter — messenger boy, newsboy, clerk, timekeeper, yardman, machine operator, and stevedore. He finally became an operative for Pinkerton's Detective Agency.

World War I, in which he served as a sergeant, interrupted his sleuthing and injured his health. When he was finally discharged from the last of several hospitals, he resumed detective work. Subsequently he turned to writing, and in the late 1920s he became the unquestioned master of detective-story fiction in America. During World War II, Mr. Hammett again served as a sergeant in the Army, this time for over two years, most of which was spent in the Aleutians. He died in 1961.

A NOTE ON THE TYPE

This book was set in Janson. The hot-metal version of Janson was a recutting made direct from type cast from matrices long thought to have been made by the Dutchman Anton Janson, who was a practicing type founder in Leipzig during the years 1668–1687. However, it has been conclusively demonstrated that these types are actually the work of Nicholas Kis (1650–1702), a Hungarian, who most probably learned his trade from the master Dutch type founder Dirk Voskens. The type is an excellent example of the influential and sturdy Dutch types that prevailed in England up to the time William Caslon (1692–1766) developed his own incomparable designs from them.

Composed by The Sarabande Press,
New York, New York

Printed and bound by
Fairfield Graphics, Fairfield, Pennsylvania

Designed by Marysarah Quinn